On Kiki's Reef

By Carol L. Malnor ◆ Illustrated by Trina L. Hunner

Dawn Publications

For all those who love the coral reef and its fascinating creatures. — CLM

For Mom and Dad —TLH

Library of Congress Cataloging-in-Publication Data
Malnor, Carol.
  Kiki's reef / by Carol L. Malnor ; illustrated by Trina L. Hunner. -- First edition.
      pages cm
  Summary: "A green sea turtle hatches and grows up in the ocean, then moves to shallower water near a coral reef where she spends most of the rest of her life. Includes supplementary information about turtles, coral reef creatures, maps, and activities"-- Provided by the publisher.
  ISBN 978-1-58469-476-2 (hardback) -- ISBN 978-1-58469-477-9 (pbk.) 1. Sea turtles--Juvenile fiction. [1. Sea turtles--Fiction. 2. Turtles--Fiction.] I. Hunner, Trina L., illustrator. II. Title.
  PZ10.3.M2967Ki 2014
  [E]--dc23
                                    2013026701

Book design and computer production by Patty Arnold, Menagerie Design & Publishing
Manufactured by Regent Publishing Services, Hong Kong
Printed January, 2014, in ShenZhen, Guangdong, China

10 9 8 7 6 5 4 3 2 1
First Edition

DAWN PUBLICATIONS
12402 Bitney Springs Road
Nevada City, CA 95959
530-274-7775
nature@dawnpub.com

A baby green sea turtle pops her head out of the sand. It's Kiki! She just hatched from her egg buried deep below.

Kiki scrambles across the beach with her brothers and sisters.

Birds try to peck them.
Crabs try to grab them.
Some never make it to the water.

Kiki does!

Surf and spray carry Kiki away.

She paddles wildly. The wide, open ocean is a big place
for a little turtle.

She searches for food and hides from big fish that would
swallow her in one bite. Kiki is smart and brave.

Kiki paddles helter-skelter.
Beds of seaweed give her shelter.

After surviving in the open ocean for six birthdays, Kiki is larger.

Her shell is brighter.
Her flippers are stronger.

She's big enough to search for a new home closer to shore. Colors and shapes swirl beneath her in the shallow water.

In the water down below,
A rainbow of corals puts on a show.

It's a coral reef!

Corals look like plants, but they're not. They're animals!

But they're not like any animals Kiki has seen before. Some look like fans. Others look like tubes. One coral looks like a brain!

Year after year their hard skeletons build up to make a giant reef—a magical underwater island.

Kiki explores!

Kiki's birthdays come and go.
Kiki's body grows and grows.

All the while she watches the
unusual creatures living on
the reef.

She sees fish of all sizes
And lots of surprises.

Zig . . . zag! Dash in . . . dart out!

A clownfish snuggles into the dangerous tentacles of an anemone. Will it get hurt? No! The clownfish wears a slimy coat to protect it from the anemone's painful stings.

Every clownfish has its own anemone, and these two are perfect partners.

In and out and all around
Lots of teamwork can be found.

Kiki discovers
some partners for
herself—a gang of tangs!
The tangs get a free lunch by eating
the algae growing on Kiki's shell. And with a
clean, smooth shell, Kiki glides through the
water with ease.

Nearby wrasses are expert cleaners too! Kiki watches
them do a wiggly dance that announces,
"Our cleaning station is open!" A grouper swims
up to be their first customer.

When a grouper opens wide,
Then a wrasse can clean inside.

Not all open mouths on the reef are friendly. The razor sharp teeth of a giant barracuda are deadly for many reef fish.

Kiki isn't afraid—she's too big for a barracuda.

But she's not too big for an approaching tiger shark!

Kiki knows so very well
A shark's strong jaws can crack her shell.

Kiki makes a quick getaway through the seagrass. When the shark is gone, she'll return to the reef.

Meanwhile, a seahorse uses a different strategy to stay safe from predators—camouflage!

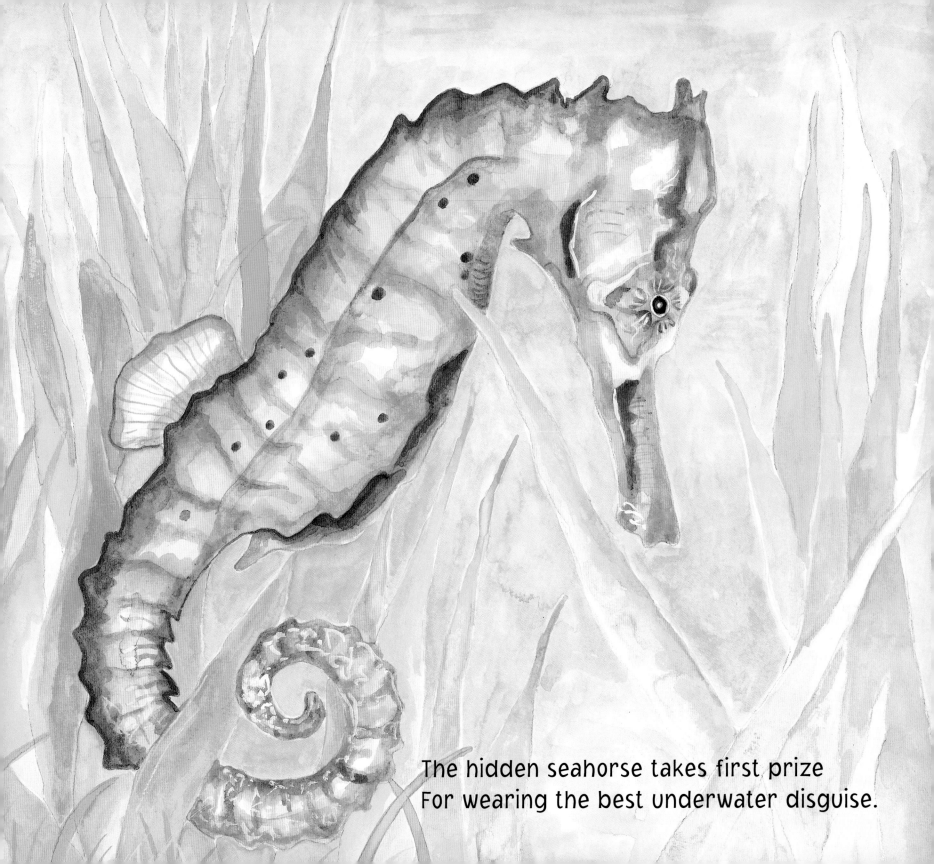

The hidden seahorse takes first prize
For wearing the best underwater disguise.

Back home on the reef, Kiki hears "crunch, crunch, crunch."

It's the sound of the sharp teeth of a parrotfish
scraping the hard coral for food.

Every bite of reef it scoops
Turns to sand when it poops.

While Kiki snoozes, nighttime creatures slither and crawl from their hiding places. A hungry octopus hunts for its dinner.

Who will it be?

A shrimp or snail or maybe a crab —
Whatever eight long arms can grab.

Kiki's happily at home on her coral reef. She knows all of the plants and animals. And they all know her and her gentle ways.

When a stranger arrives, curious Kiki swims over to investigate.

A diver visits this magical place
And meets a turtle face-to-face.

Then one day Kiki feels different inside. Somehow she knows it's time to return to her first home—the beach. She takes off on a journey of hundreds of miles.

Along the way, a fishing boat pulls a net through the water. Kiki can't get out of the way in time. She gets caught!

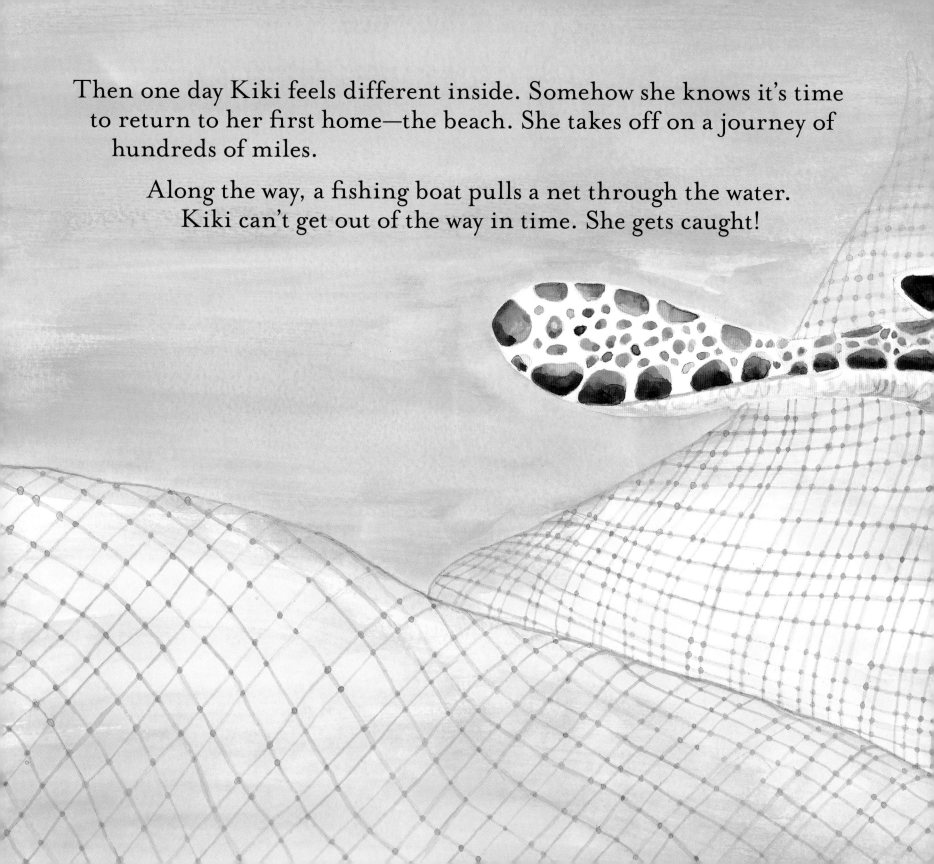

Escaping through
the net's trap door,

Lucky Kiki
swims toward shore.

In the middle of the night, Kiki hauls her
heavy body across the same beach where she was
born. Using her back flippers like a shovel, she
digs a deep nest and lays a hundred eggs.

They'll hatch into baby green sea turtles—just like
she did so many years ago.

Carefully covering the eggs, Kiki's work is done.
She drags herself back into the sea and silently
swims away in the moonlight.

Along the coast and through the foam,
Kiki returns to her reef home.

Featured Creatures

A coral reef is an amazing habitat where spectacular sea creatures live and die, compete and cooperate. *On Kiki's Reef* features a sampling of the variety of sea animals that can be found at reefs around the world.

Surf and spray carry Kiki away.

During their long lives (over 80 years) green sea turtles go through several stages.

Hatchlings—Green sea turtle hatchlings, only two inches long, instinctively scurry toward the natural light of the ocean on the horizon. Although some are eaten by crabs, birds, and other predators, many make it to the water and frantically swim out to giant beds of sargassum seaweed. They float in the open ocean up to ten years feeding on small plants and animals.

Juveniles—When a green sea turtle has grown to the size of a dinner plate, six to ten years old, it swims to shallower water, often near a reef, and begins to feed exclusively on sea grass and algae. Living on green plants causes its fat to become tinted green. It gets its name from the color of its fat, not the color of its heart-shaped shell, which is mottled shades of brown, olive, and red.

Adults—When full-grown, adult green sea turtles are three to five feet long and weigh 150 to 350 pounds. They spend their lives in warm ocean waters all over the world. They reach sexual maturity between 20 and 50 years old and migrate to mate near the beaches where they were born. A female turtle lays about 100 golf ball sized eggs at a time in several nests about every two years. She returns to her feeding area and never sees her young. Only about one out of 1,000 hatchlings survive to adulthood.

A rainbow of corals puts on a show.

One of the most amazing things about a coral reef is that it's alive. It may look like rock, but the surface of the reef is covered with a layer of living coral. Corals are tiny animals called polyps. They have a tube-shaped body with a mouth at the top that's surrounded by tentacles. A type of algae (zooxanthellae) lives inside their tissues, providing them with energy and nutrients and giving them beautiful colors. Because algae need warmth and light to grow, coral reefs are found in clear, shallow water.

There are two kinds of corals: hard and soft. Each hard coral polyp builds a cup-shaped skeleton at its base to protect its fragile body. The coral polyp retreats into its skeleton during the day and comes out at night to eat. When polyps die, their skeletons form the foundation for new polyps to grow. Brain, branching, star, tube, and table corals are some of the many types of hard corals. Layers of their skeletons form a coral reef. Individual coral polyps are at most an eighth of an inch in size, but the coral reefs they build are the largest living structures on earth. Soft corals, like sea fans, live on the reef, but don't make skeletons.

Coral reefs are called the "rainforests of the ocean" because they support such a vast diversity of plants and animals. Some animals are permanent residents on the reef and never leave. Others use the reef like an oasis, stopping by to eat and rest. Green sea turtles use coral reefs as feeding areas, grazing the reef for algae and eating seagrass that grows nearby.

Lots of teamwork can be found.

Clownfish and anemones are well-known partners. Working together as a team, they protect each other and share food. Anemones are meat-eating animals that use their venomous tentacles to paralyze fish and then eat them. However, the clownfish can dash in and out of the anemone's tentacles for safety and protection without being hurt.

In return, the clownfish chases away the anemone's enemies. The anemone also eats bits of food the clownfish drops. This kind of partnership is called *symbiosis*.

Our cleaning station is open!

Even though sea turtles and fish live in water, they get "dirty" with algae, bacteria, and parasites. They can't clean themselves, so they get a "bath" at a cleaning station—places on the coral reef where special cleaner fish congregate. While yellow tangs clean green sea turtles, bluestreak wrasses have a partnership with bigger fish, such as tomato groupers. Tiny wrasses can even swim inside the grouper's mouth without fear of being eaten.

Not all open mouths on the reef are friendly.

The mouth of a great barracuda is filled with two sets of dagger-like teeth. Hovering around the reef with its mouth half open, this fierce predator watches for prey. It swallows small prey whole, but rips and tears larger prey into pieces to eat separately. Barracudas typically eat fish, octopus, and shrimp. They'll also eat young green sea turtles, but fully-grown turtles are too big for them.

A shark's strong jaws can crack her shell.

Growing to 13 feet, the tiger shark is a "top" predator on the coral reef. It uses its keen eyesight and a highly developed sense of smell to locate prey. With rows of razor-sharp teeth and powerful jaws, tiger sharks aren't picky eaters. Scientists have found the remains of dolphins, stingrays, fish, seals, birds, and even license plates and old tires in their stomachs. Tiger sharks, along with humans, are the main predators of sea turtles.

First prize for wearing the best underwater disguise.

A seahorse is a master of camouflage. Its ability to change color to blend in with its surroundings is a good defense against predators, such as crabs, fish, and rays. Although it doesn't look it, a seahorse is actually a fish. It uses its long tail to cling to coral or anchor itself to seagrass. Seagrasses are one of the main types of plants growing in the coral reef ecosystem and are a major source of food for adult green sea turtles.

Every bite of reef it scoops, turns to sand when it poops.

Parrotfish scoop and scrape the reef with a parrot-like beak in order to get the algae that grow on top of the reef and inside coral polyps. Parrotfish use the algae for nutrition, but can't digest the coral, which is turned to powder as it passes through the fish's digestive system. The powder is deposited (pooped) back into the ocean as white coral sand. One large parrotfish makes about a ton of sand a year!

Whatever eight long arms can grab!

An octopus has eight arms. Each one, lined with two rows of suction cups, can stretch out in all directions to grab prey. The suction cups are equipped with special sensors so the octopus can taste what it's touching. They hunt at night and will eat anything that strays into their path. If an eel or a shark grabs them by an arm, the octopus has the ability to release the arm and escape. Over time the arm will grow back.

Carol's Teaching Treasures

KIKI IS A GREEN SEA TURTLE, one of seven species of turtles that live in the world's oceans. Other species are loggerhead, leatherback, hawksbill, olive ridley, Kemp's ridley, and flatback. Most sea turtle species are considered either threatened or endangered. However, early childhood is not a time for children to focus on environmental problems. It's a time for bonding with nature. As nature educator David Sobel advises, "No tragedies before fourth grade." Toward that end, *On Kiki's Reef* sparks young children's curiosity about the magical world of the coral reef, while it nurtures their love and appreciation for sea life, especially turtles. Once children make a heartfelt connection with sea turtles, caring for them will naturally follow.

Seven Species Same and Different

Although all sea turtles are similar in some ways, each species has unique characteristics. Using photos from the sources listed below, invite children to use their observation skills to notice similarities and differences among sea turtle species. The class may work together to create a chart, or individual students can compare two species by making a Venn diagram.

- Sea Turtle Conservancy—http://www.conserveturtles.org (click on Educator's Corner; Turtle Tides)
- N.E.S.T.—http://www.nestonline.org (click on Turtle Facts; Sea Turtle Information)
- SEE Turtles—www.seeturtles.org (click on Sea Turtle Facts)

Before and After

As a pre-reading activity, show children the page in the book where Kiki "sees fish of all sizes and lots of surprises." Ask them to point out the sea creatures Kiki sees and identify the ones they know. Throughout the story, children will learn about these featured creatures. After reading Kiki's story, go back to this page to review each creature. Share information from "Featured Creatures" to add to the children's understanding.

Scavenger Hunt

The coral reef is full of diversity, including the following page of "Illustrious Additions." Show children the illustrations and share the information in your own words. Then ask them to find these sea creatures swimming on the pages throughout the book. You'll notice that these creatures are listed in alphabetical order, not in their order of appearance in the book.

People Helping Turtles

Although people can hurt turtles, they can also help them. Kiki was able to escape from a fishing net because of a clever invention called a Turtle Excluder Device (TED). Use these resources for more information about the TED and other ways people are helping turtles:

- Learn how TED saves turtles www.nmfs.noaa.gov/pr/species/turtles/teds.htm
- Adopt a Turtle at www.seaturtle.org/adopt or www.conserveturtles.org (click on Adopt)
- Read a biography of Archie Carr "The Scientist Who Saved Sea Turtles" in *Earth Heroes: Champions of the Ocean* by Fran Hodgkins (Dawn Publications, 2009).

Treasure Chest of Lessons

- *Teacher's Guide to A Swim Through the Sea* by Carol L. Malnor (Dawn Publications, 1998) offers lesson plans for a diversity of ocean plants and animals, including clownfish, sea turtles, angelfish, and many more.
- More activities for this book, including the game "Race to the Sea," are available at the publisher's website, www.dawnpub.com. Click on "Activities" and scroll to this book to download lesson plans and additional teacher resources.
- NOAA Coral Reef Conservation—Find a variety of activities, including simple experiments, puzzles, and games. http://coralreef.noaa.gov/education/educators/resourcecd/activities/

In addition to the featured creatures, Kiki swims with interesting and unusual creatures illustrated throughout the story.

Illustrious Additions

Batwing Coral Crab—These small crabs hide in the crevices and cavities of the reef during the day and come out at night. They help keep the reef healthy by eating dead material and removing dirt and sediment that settles around the corals.

Bicolor Anthias—The body of this anthias is divided into two colors (bicolor)—one color on top and a different color on the bottom. Hundreds of bicolor anthias swim in schools around coral reefs. They all begin life as females, but one female changes to become a male and rules over the other females.

Chestnut Turbo Snail—There are thousands of species of reef snails, and no two species have shells exactly the same shape or color. By grazing on reef algae, reef snails help keep the reef clean and healthy.

Feather Duster Worm—Sea worms are related to earthworms, but are a lot more colorful. The tentacles on top of feather duster worms extend into the water to filter food. When threatened, the worms quickly withdraw deep into their tube homes.

Ghost Crab—This land crab doesn't live on the reef, but on a sandy beach. It burrows into the sand to hide during the day, and comes out at night to hunt for food. It eats sea turtle eggs as well as little sea turtle hatchlings.

Raccoon Butterflyfish—There are over 100 different species of butterflyfish, all wearing different colors and patterns. Their disc-shaped bodies are thin and flat, similar to their cousins the angelfish. The raccoon butterflyfish is named for the black mask across its face.

Red Night Shrimp—These shrimp hide in the reef during the day and come out at night to eat. Their huge eyes allow them to see in almost complete darkness. When a diver's light shines on them, their eyes look like red dots glowing in the black water.

Reef Triggerfish—This is the official state fish of Hawaii. It's fun to try to pronounce it's Hawaiian name, taking it one syllable at a time: Hu-mu-hu-mu-nu-ku-nu-ku-a-pu-a'a. The translation into English is "fish that grunts like a pig,"

Spotted Eagle Stingray—Gracefully flying through the water, the stingray flaps the sides of its body like big wings. It's called a stingray because it has a long tail with venomous spines. Stingrays don't have any bones in their bodies, just cartilage. Cartilage is the same material that you feel inside the tip of your nose and ears.

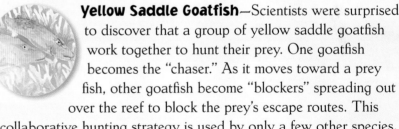

Yellow Saddle Goatfish—Scientists were surprised to discover that a group of yellow saddle goatfish work together to hunt their prey. One goatfish becomes the "chaser." As it moves toward a prey fish, other goatfish become "blockers" spreading out over the reef to block the prey's escape routes. This collaborative hunting strategy is used by only a few other species, such as chimps, orcas, dolphins, and lions.

Coral reefs are found in tropical and subtropical oceans near coastlines all around the world. Millions of species live on coral reefs, but not every species lives in every ocean. However, the species illustrated on each page of *On Kiki's Reef* live together in the wild.

Photo by Bruce Malnor

Carol Malnor has used personal experiences to spark her many writing adventures. A mystical experience on a coral reef inspired her to choose the ocean as the setting for *On Kiki's Reef*. In a previous book, *Molly's Organic Farm*, Carol drew on her homesteading experience in Michigan's north woods. She tapped into her passion for birding to co-author *The BLUES Go Birding* picture books series. As a retired teacher, Carol wrote the kind of biographies she wanted to give her students when she co-authored the *Earth Heroes* biographical series with her husband, Bruce. Several teacher's guides grew out of her personal experience using Dawn Publications' books in her classroom. Currently Carol writes a blog for teachers and parents at www.insideoutsidenature.com. Find her nature inspirations and workshop information on her website www.natureportals.com.

Photo by Melanie Soleil

Even though she is landlocked in the Western Sierra Nevadas, Trina Hunner tries to swim with sea turtles every chance she gets. Her favorite experience was looking into the eyes of a beautiful sea turtle while swimming in a coral reef in Kauai. When she isn't swimming in the sea she enjoys biking and skiing in the mountains near her home. She lives with her husband Nikos and their two cats in Nevada City, California. Trina illustrated *Molly's Organic Farm* for Dawn Publications, a book based on her experience with a homeless cat on a neighboring community farm. To see more of her artwork you can visit her website, www.trinahunner.com.

Other Books by Carol L. Malnor

Molly's Organic Farm is based on the true story of a homeless cat that found herself in the wondrous world of an organic farm. Seen through Molly's eyes, the reader discovers the interplay of nature that grows wholesome food.

The BLUES Go Birding Series (co-authored with Sandy Fuller) — Three books that introduce birds to young children. The information is accurate and useful for a young birder, and presented with a generous helping of humor:

> *The BLUES Go Birding Across America*
> *The BLUES Go Birding At Wild*
>   *America's Shores*
> *The BLUES Go Extreme Birding*

The Earth Heroes Series — Each of these books for middle school children presents the biographies of eight of the world's greatest naturalists, with special attention not only to their careers and lasting contributions, but also to events in their youth that foreshadowed greatness:

> *Earth Heroes: Champions of the Wilderness*
> *Earth Heroes: Champions of Wild Animals*

Other Books from Dawn Publications

Granny's Clan — Life as a wild orca (killer) whale is very much a family affair. Here is the true story of Granny, a 100 year-old whale matriarch, and how she teaches young whales and helps her magnificent clan to survive.

In the Trees, Honey Bees offers an inside-the-hive view of a wild colony, along with solid information about these remarkable and valuable creatures.

The "Over" Series — Kids sing and clap, thinking these books are entertainment, while adults think they are educational! Patterned on the classic old tune of "Over in the Meadow," this series by Marianne Berkes includes *Over in the Ocean, Over in the Jungle, Over in the Arctic, Over in the Forest, Over in a River*, and *Over in Australia*.

The "Mini-Habitat" Series — Beginning with the insects to be found under a rock (*Under One Rock: Bugs, Slugs and Other Ughs*) and moving on to other small habitats (around old logs, on flowers, cattails, cactuses, and in a tidepool), author Anthony Fredericks has a flair for introducing children to interesting "neighborhoods" of creatures. Field trips between covers!

The "E-I-E-I-O" Series follow the adventures of young Jo, granddaughter of Old MacDonald, as she discovers the delights of the pond, woods, and garden on Old MacDonald's farm. E—I—E—I—O!

> *Jo MacDonald Saw a Pond*
> *Jo MacDonald Hiked in the Woods*
> *Jo MacDonald Had a Garden.*

Dawn Publications is dedicated to inspiring in children a deeper understanding and appreciation for all life on Earth. You can browse through our titles, download resources for teachers, and order at www.dawnpub.com or call 800-545-7475.

Coral Reefs of the World

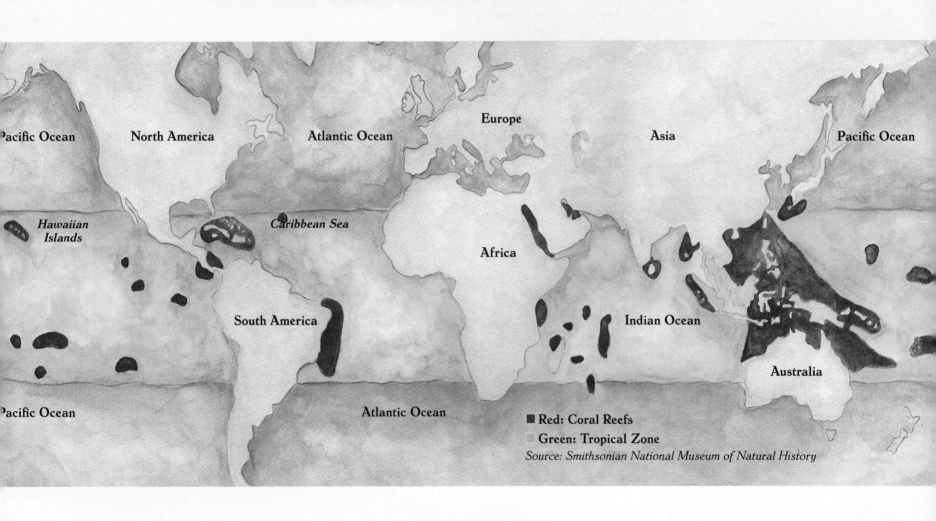

Pacific Ocean   North America   Atlantic Ocean   Europe   Asia   Pacific Ocean

Hawaiian Islands   *Caribbean Sea*   Africa

South America   Indian Ocean   Australia

Pacific Ocean   Atlantic Ocean

■ Red: Coral Reefs
■ Green: Tropical Zone
Source: Smithsonian National Museum of Natural History